Kenzie,

I hope you really enjoy reading this book!

Thanks for being here when it arrived.

love,

J

Drawing Love

By Juli Jousan

Illustrations by Katrina Binkewicz

An Indie Writers Press Book

Copyright © 2010 by Juli Jousan

Copyright © 2010 Illustrations by Katrina Binkewicz

Printed in China

Indie Writers Press

P.O. Box 6689

Ithaca, NY 14851

ISBN 0615401732

First Edition

"Maybe the lines I drew were always lines to them, threads of connection to the sounds of their voices, the scents of the foods they ate for breakfast."

-Juli Jousan

Drawing Love

The most important thing that happened in Amsterdam was that I opened my black and white marble Mead notebook; the pages were thick and wavy from the time I went walking in the rain.

The first page read:

It all comes in like rapids, like spaghetti, Snickers bars, or too much cheesecake. I can fit no more. I hate my new high school. I feel tight, nervous, and locked up. It's the slowest February in my history. The more I want the thaw, the longer they draw it out. Wait. Wait. Wait. Freeze.

I signed up for a school play. It might make spring come faster. Then I can be outside. Outside is my religion.

"Memorize: paramecium, euglena, xylum, phloem, and the Pythagorean Theorem. Be certain that you put your commas in the correct places. It doesn't matter what you say, just as long as I find it agreeable. Oh, and be exactly here at exactly then, so I can show you exactly how to think about exactly everything. Be on time."

That's how all my teachers sound, and they know how to drag out time like biting down hard can make a small piece of taffy a long one with a good pull. They don't see why there are lines from songs written all over note books. They have no idea why my crazy short black hair flies

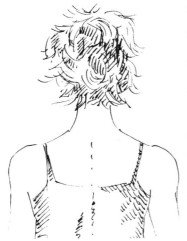

everywhere; it sticks out in at least seventeen different directions, sometimes more. My best moments could probably be scientifically monitored and documented by the unruliness of my half curls. The wilder my hair, the better the day.

They don't think the way I do. They stare disapprovingly at my combat boots and wish my cargo pants and t-shirts would miraculously turn *into an appropriately flowered dress.*

*They don't see the poetry. They don't
understand. Does the Pythagorean Theorem
understand that Christmas trees
lose their dried-up needles and
pumpkins get rotten and smelly
when it's past their season? Do
xylem and phloem understand
how my father is drowning in gin and
tonics?*

There were thousands of bicycles in Amsterdam. There were red-wax wheels of Gouda cheese and wooden clogs stacked up for visitors to buy. I wasn't a tourist; I was a student. My father had come out of his alcoholic haze long enough to make sure that I applied to colleges. My stepfather Hank signed me up for a summer abroad program. He had his reasons.

Here, across the ocean from my home, people hummed underground Dutch rock and roll on their way to the train station. In front of the museums, Dutch collided with English, French, German, and Italian. I liked Scottish accents most.

The buildings there remembered the sound of machine guns, and I imagined screams were still trapped between bricks. The war seemed so much a part of the present in Amsterdam, like it still lived and you could taste it in the car exhaust.

It was the old life and the new life, the inhale and exhale of Amsterdam, and it was mine for the whole summer. The streets made of water made me think that even I could grow to like living in a city. I wanted their foreignness to be my everyday thing, my world beyond Dad and Samantha.

I read for my art class. The first week I was there, I got a small crush on a sculpture of a naked woman. Or maybe I fell in love with the fact that I was allowed to look at her without pretending that I wasn't. There were lots of lovely ladies and landscapes in the museums. The Rijksmuseum, the van Gogh, and the Stedalijk were just the beginning.

I stood in front of van Gogh's "Plain d'Anvers." I love that painting, the brush strokes in the field, the sky. I wanted to reach in and run my fingers through the grass, through the still wet paint.

I met a kid named Jimmy in the park across the street from the school. We smoked a joint together and talked about his brother's record collection. His brother has enough albums to fill a room, or so Jimmy says. All his brother has is records, a stereo, and a bed.

Jimmy has short brown hair that he keeps pretty neat most of the time. He's big, like a football player. He seems pretty normal until you start up a conversation with him. He talks really, really fast. I don't think his family has much money because his clothes are too big or small on him. A girl in my English class said, "He's missing something," and she knocked her head with her palm and said, "...here." He's missing something, but who isn't? He can really play the guitar, probably better than me.

At play rehearsal, this tall girl with blue eyes and long blond hair talked to me. Her name is Samantha. It was special from the first moment. I knew it by the way she looked at me and by the way we talked.

I had her over to my new stepfather's house. Jimmy came over too.

I told them how we moved from my dad's

house in Leonia to Hank's house in Tenafly, from real people to plastic ones, from a real house with peeling paint and old garage sale bookshelves to interior decoration and hard cover novels resting on pure oak. It makes me want to roll around in a mud puddle. Jimmy laughed when I told him that. I showed them my guitars, and I told them about the band I want to start. I showed them the swimming pool, the tennis court, and the place my mother's garden will be. I told them how I wish all the land was wild and there weren't any roads, only pathways and trees. We climbed my favorite tree in the yard, it's a big old oak, and we smoked. Jimmy said he wants to jam.

Samantha's a senior, a year older than me. I've seen her eyes up close now. They are very blue, tie-dyed. She is the type that would lie in bed on a rainy Saturday reading fairy tales and sipping raspberry tea. She is water colored.

Today I walked into John's room. He was sitting on the floor leaning up against the wall. Across the room, he had all Dad's empty booze bottles lined up on the floor next to the wall. He shot at them with his BB gun. Glass was shattering everywhere.

The whisper yells are starting. It's like I'm back in the old house. Their room is next to mine and I can hear Mom and Dad trying to make their angry whispers be a secret. They try not to let me know, but I can hear them then, and I can hear them now. The whisper yells are starting. My closet is talking. Tap, tap, tapping like little fingers. Long nails tap. The monster under my bed is shifting.

I thought being sixteen would make the monsters go away. I thought being sixteen would stop the tapping.

In Amsterdam, I played my acoustic guitar on the dirty sidewalk in front of the University. I needed to see where my music was going without Jimmy, so I played without him to the people who walked by, and to the summer. One day I wrote a song while I performed. It felt like climbing a tree. It was open and natural, and all about her. It was all about Samantha. Her hair was in my strings, her eyes looked into mine; the ocean between us wasn't working.

"Get up off the canvas and kiss me," I kept singing. It was a song about the Mona Lisa, and how she had been loved so much on canvas, surrounded for years by admirers, that all that love had brought her back to life. It was what I wanted to happen to Samantha's love. I wanted it to come the hell down from its suspended state. I wanted it moving.

I almost took the way out by water, bags packed. John and I slept out at the lake, near our summer house in New Hampshire. Some kids there had invited us to go, so we went. I don't remember how many bottles of wine we drank or how much green New Hampshire weed we smoked. I do remember the moon rising over the navy blue hill. I remember throwing bugs into a spider's web.

We all got naked and jumped into the lake. I remember the water felt warm, and I dove deep. But then I didn't know which way was up. I didn't know which blackness held the stars.

I scrambled hard to get a grip on the water; I frantically grabbed handfuls and handfuls.

The next thing I knew, I was coughing and puking wine and lake water, and John was on the dock next to me crying. He had pulled me out.

The dormitory I lived in at the University of Amsterdam looked like an old stone castle. It was built in the fifteenth century. On my way to class, I thought, *once carriages drove past, now cars*. I wondered what would replace the castle building when it finally deteriorated and fell to the ground. Everything would change.

When Professor Everitt first walked into the classroom, I was sure she was exactly like my mother. Her pumps, the tasteful highlights in her age-appropriate short hair, and her southwestern Virginia accent made me wonder why I'd traveled so far. I could have heard everything she was about to say in my own living room. Why didn't I have a Dutch professor? Why did the professor from the small school I had gotten into have to teach the class?

She began, "Art is a vast world with as many possibilities as the human being herself. In this class we can only hope to begin scratching the surface. To truly learn something, you will work harder in here than in any other class you have taken. Since I create the syllabus as

 we go, you will have to stay caught up. No learning everything the night before you take the final exam and forgetting it the next day. For this class, you will spend long hours reading historical texts as well as whole Saturdays working on drawings. If you are here to waste time on an elective that doesn't mean anything to you, then drop the class now. If you have decided in two weeks that you can't learn anything from me, drop the class." She paused. "If you want to learn something about art, you are in the right place. Any questions?"

Professor Everitt was not my mother, but like my mother, she wasn't going to be easy to deal with. She assigned an entire book to be read that week.

She lectured that day about how Michelangelo was both a painter and a sculptor. This comforted me. Guitar, drawing, painting, sculpture. I played and painted. He painted and sculpted. I figured I would be all right, because I loved both. Sometimes drawing gave me a lump in my throat, but I never hated it. Professor Everitt said Michelangelo had opened up a new door. Then she started talking about doorways large and small. She talked about finding paths to entirely new genres of art; she mentioned Jackson Pollack. She explained that for each drawing a person must find a doorway of vision to begin creating the "room" of the image—something beyond the doorway.

I had never heard anyone teach like that. I was used to falling asleep in classes. I was used to teachers never knowing what they were talking about. I spent class time in high school thinking about Samantha or watching the clock tick at a horrifyingly slow rate, but Dr. Everitt's class was alive. I ate it like Oreo cookies with whipped cream. Everything Dr. Everitt said, she said with intention. Every moment I felt like she was coming out with an important thought that I needed to write down in my notebook. It was like a sermon to me. For once in my life, the person in front of the room was actually a teacher. Hank had been right. I realized I could learn something. I cared what grade I got. I wanted Dr. Everitt to know I was different. I also wanted her to see if I was good; I wanted to know if I could really draw. I was willing to work for her.

"CAN I DRAW FROM MY BEGINNING?"

That was the thought for the week that she wrote on the board. I knew I could play my guitar that way. I could play right out of God. The music came from the soul of me, and I didn't need to work too hard at that. Drawing was different. The paper was further from the source. I wanted to it to be close, right there. I wanted to feel my pencil touch the page like love.

As I sat there listening and thinking in a new way, I

watched her walk up and down the aisles of the classroom—in between the drawing tables. She was tightly woven; the bands of muscles in her legs and back gripped one another so they would not burst.

At the end of the class, Dr. Everitt assigned three chapters to read in our textbook, and then she started walking out the door, stopped, turned back to the class and said, "I also want you to draw a doorway." Then she left.

That afternoon, after reading two chapters for my class, I pulled out my notebook.

Sam came over Sunday afternoon. It was one of the first warm days since fall. Mom and Hank were out at a cocktail party, so we took a bottle of their wine down into the bottom of the empty pool.

It was greater than great to be outside. It was sunny, and half the pool was pretty dry. In the deep end there was a small pond of melted snow.

Samantha wore a button-down white shirt. The thin line of lace next to the delicate buttons is all I have been able to think about since then. Her long elegant legs stretching out on the pool floor repeat themselves again and again in my mind.

She was buzzed from the wine, and the ideas came out of her like flower bouquets or bowls of candy on Halloween. She talked about how everyone is expected to be the same in this world. "They want everyone to be a certain way, and when someone is different it scares them. They will judge you right out of existence if you let them," she said.

She is all I can think about.

On the weekend, most of the students from the U.S. went to the hash bars or off to Paris. I stayed in Amsterdam and read for Dr. Everitt. I played my acoustic on the sidewalks next an artist named Jan, who did chalk drawings on the sidewalk at the entrance to the Metro. Jan wore jeans from head to toe—jean pants, jean shirts, and a blue denim hat. He smelled like sweat and manliness. He didn't talk much, but he learned my songs and sang with me sometimes. And then there was thunder singing with me in the dense heat. Raindrops fell inside my guitar, and Jimmy's song dissolved into the hot air. And with denser rain, Jan's drawing disappeared into the sidewalk.

"Molly," Mom said, "Let's go get some ice cream."

I could tell she just needed to get out of the house.

"O.K., I'll go."

I didn't feel like putting my shoes on, so when we got to the store, my feet were bare.

"Molly Taylor, you can't go in without shoes."

"They won't notice," I said.

"Put your shoes on."

"They're not with me."

"It's still practically winter."

"Let's just get the ice cream."

"You wait here," she said.

"I want to pick out the flavor."

"Get back in the car."

"I'll do what I want."

"You will not, young lady. Wait right here."

I ran right to the ice cream freezer and grabbed a half gallon of chocolate. My mother came down the aisle looking long; her anger made her tall. She took the ice cream out of my hands and walked toward the register. "You will eat none of this," she said to a wall of cereal.

I bolted out of the store and up the street, and as soon as she paid the bill she followed me in Hank's blue Mercedes.

She found me on Wade Street, pulled up close, and rolled down her electric window. I was still running, and she drove next to me.

"Get in the car, Molly. Come on." She followed me for a minute. "Please," she said to me nicely.

"Let me walk home."

"Not without shoes."

"You hate my boots. I would think you would be happy that they are at home in my closet."

She stopped the car, and I thought about running across the grass and away from her.... My feet really were frozen, so I got into the car.

"Can't we ever just have a nice family evening?"

"Are we a family?" I asked.

"Of course we are."

"Hank will never be my family."

Was I an artist or a musician? Was I the notes I played, the songs I wrote, or was I the lines I made with my pencil? Or were the notes the touches of my lover?

Or was I without Samantha? Was I a lack of her? Was that all I was? Was I Dadless, without a father—was that all of who I was? Maybe the lines I drew were always lines to them, threads of connection to the sounds of their voices, the scents of the foods they ate for breakfast. I brought my notebook, but I also brought a drawing pad full of pictures I'd drawn of her all the way to Europe. And I added to them every day. It was the only way I had left to touch her. I stayed close by drawing Samantha. Drawing was a way to keep what was gone, a way to shrink the loss.

I closed my eyes and I could smell her—vanilla extract and sweet skin. I knew a part of her was still with me.

I run ten countries ragged

Tatter the flag –

Chasing love across the fjords and over rocky

Seas –

In trains, cars, and buses,

I chase my love.

It's always hard to sing it,

And most of all not to sing,

Not to run the country ragged,

Not to shred the flag,

not to chase the kiss

of my love.

After play rehearsal last night, I went over to Samantha's house. Her father, Mr. Thompson, wears wire rim glasses, and he has a professor's brain. Mrs. Thompson is a sweet, cookie baking mother.

Samantha's parents get along almost too well. At dinner they were formal, and they were really nice to me. They even asked me about my music and listened to ten whole minutes of my rock and roll talk.

"If there was no music to rock the younger generations, how would they ever make it through high school?" I asked. "And movies, painting, and plays—what would people do if they couldn't see all of the possibilities that the artists created for them? Maybe it's the artists' job to remind people that life is possible." That thought made me want to play the guitar. The thought that I can help someone

24

remember they are alive makes me want to write an epic rock and roll opera.

Samantha told them I was going to be a great musician. When she compliments me, not just my face but my whole body turns red.

After we finished eating, Samantha and I went up to her room to listen to some records. She has one of those little record players that you have when you're a little kid, and most of her albums are by folk artists like James Taylor and Cat Stevens. She also has records from Broadway musicals, and their covers are tattered from being played so much.

There are books all over her room, and pens, and pencils, and a set of watercolor paints.

"Let's play with these," I said, pulling the paintbrush out.

She put "Fiddler on the Roof" on the record

player and got a cup of water out of the bathroom.

"I think we should paint your sneakers," I said, and I picked up her white canvas Van, and watched a tree grow up out of the plastic that lined the bottom. I filled the tree in with my paint, and I made it green and full and Spring. When I hold a pencil or paintbrush in my hand, the surface I'm going to work on holds the drawing; it's the secret keeper that whispers the ideas to me.

Sam made her other shoe all pink, and then she put red polka dots all over it. It looked great.

"I'm gonna have a hard time getting out of here tomorrow with these on my feet," she said.

"Just tell your mother a budding young artist painted them for you. Stress the *art* part."

Before Samantha took me home, she read me a story. I stretched out on the floor, straight out at the bottom of her bed, and Samantha was backward on the bed, with her feet on the pillow. She was belly down, the book in her hands. When I looked up at her, I could see her hair coming down around the pages like icicles dripping off a roof.

I let my back sink into the floor. As she read, I felt safe, safer than I have felt in a long time, like I didn't have to watch my back, and like I could let my thoughts rest.

Today I was home alone. Mom was downtown getting some groceries, and I found one of her old writing journals on a bookshelf. I took it into my room and read it. The writing was in blue ink on an old Tulane notebook. The first few pages were in prose, and she was talking about her philosophy teacher. I read a few more pages and found the poetry.

I read pages of Autumn leaves.

I watch color fall out.

I hold each beauty and toss it back

ten thousand times to the sky.

I read everything I could. There were pages
about Hank, who she knew in college, and pages
about her meeting Dad. She described her history
professor. She had written five pages about the first
time she had read Shakespeare. She had read
Hamlet, and she explained how she had worried
about him.

I watch her sit up nights and read, but not
Shakespeare. Now she reads about keeping
antiques beautiful and about investing money.

When she came home, I slapped her journal
down on the kitchen table and said, "Why the hell

is the only thing you wrote today a fucking grocery list?"

She stared at the book.

"Why did you stop writing?" I asked.

She placed the carton of milk she was going to put away on the counter, still staring at the notebook. "I stopped believing I could be good," she said.

I picked up the book and handed it to her.

"Then write... because you are good," I said softly. "I believe you are a good writer."

"Molly, I do my gardens now, like always. I'm raising you kids. One person only has so much energy."

"And writing..."

"Molly, you can plant a tomato and eat it. Flowers are beautiful when you plant them yourself and they grow."

"What about wildflowers, Mom, and poems?"

She paused for a moment, and I glanced at the pair of well-worn gardening gloves across the room.

"When you become an adult, you will understand that life takes over sometimes. Diapers need changing, bills need paying, and your creative expression changes."

"I think you still have talent as a writer, Mom, and John and I are out of diapers now."

"O.K., Molly. Could you ease up for once? We've had one hell of a year, and I'm sick of this battlefield."

"We're not talking about me and you. We are talking about your writing." I tried to speak calmly to her.

"O.K. Molly, O.K." She put the milk in the refrigerator.

"Mo, Mo, Mo," the soldiers keep calling in time. Their boots are falling into a marching rhythm.

"God damn it, Evelyn. What do you want from me?" Dad whisper screams.

"I just want you to listen to my story."

"Do you remember when I would creep into bed when we were first married, and you would wake up and turn the lights on and make me read what I'd written? You'd say, 'That's beautiful, Ev, read that sentence to me again.'"

"It's all me. Isn't it? Let's do it. Let's sit. I'll turn all the goddamned lights in the house on. Invite the neighbors in. Stop the world. Evelyn

Taylor is going to read."

"John, please."

John, please, please, please, please. Thump, thump, thump. Marching in battalions. Get out of my ears. Get out of me.

My parents are fighting in me.

As I walked to the fine arts building late Sunday afternoon, I took the last sip of thick black coffee. I knew it would take me all night, but I wanted to draw. I pulled Jimmy's leather jacket out of the closet of my dorm room, not because I thought I'd need it, but because I wanted him with me in Amsterdam.

I walked into the room and I took out my drawing pad and pencils. About half of Dr. Everitt's class was in the room focusing on our assignment, so involved in their work that only one girl looked up from her drawing to say hello.

The radio was on; it sounded like Arabic music.

I opened up my pad and began drawing a stone wall with a wooden doorway. I planned to cover the wall with ivy and leave the door cracked open, revealing a garden of flowers on the other side. I started filling the entire page with stones.

I kept thinking, "Happiness is on the other side of the door," and I breathed in deeply to catch the scent of flowers drifting through the small opening in the thick wooden door.

It took me an hour to draw three or four stones, and around nine o'clock I went outside for a cigarette. I walked out of the building into the night. It was light, city night light that made an endless day, like being on the rooftops downtown with Jimmy back home. The trees on campus were green. There was a chill, a breeze that blew in off the ocean, so I pulled the leather together over my breasts.

Saturday night when I finally found him, Jimmy was hanging out downtown in the store on the corner. He was playing pinball, and I snuck up on him from behind.

"Want to get high?"

He jumped.

"Jesus, Mo, you scared the crap out of me."

"How ya doin'?" I asked.

"Fine, now I know you're not a cop."

"Do I, Mo Taylor, look like a cop?"

"No," he said, laughing.

I needed to get high, so we walked around the corner into the alley and climbed up an old ladder onto the roof of the grocery store. It was cold, but looking down on the lights made it feel warmer to me.

I had rolled some joints the day before, and they were sitting in the almost-empty pack of cigarettes I had been smoking all day. There were three of them.

"So, James, I see you're wearing your leather. That's a cool jacket, man." I lit the first joint.

"You can wear it sometimes. Only you, Mo."

I sucked in my smoke with my words, "I'd like that, Jimmy. How about now?"

I handed him the joint, and he took two long drags. He looked over the long green trench coat I was wearing.

"This is a Mod jacket, man, like the Mods in Quadrophenia."

"No shit, Mo. I know what it is," he said.

"Oh, that's what I wanted to talk to you

about, playing 'Sea and Sand' off *Quadrophenia*. Doing anything off that album, really."

"I'll work on it. I'll get the song book," he said.

"That album says how it feels. I started to sing, 'Here by the sea and sand, nothing ever goes as planned.'"

He smiled. "I'll listen more," he said, as he sucked up the last of the joint, and I lit the next one. It was too cold to feel high yet.

"So what do you say?" I took off my jacket and handed it to him. He took it with the joint. "I'm freezing man, what do you say?"

"Fuck," he said, and put the joint in his mouth like a cigarette. He threw my jacket down on the roof, and he took off his own, and he handed it to me. He put on my jacket, took a hit, and handed the joint back to me.

"This feels good," I said, putting on his leather. "How do I look?"

He laughed again. "You look great, and I am a sucker. I will kill you if anything happens to that jacket. I will kill you." And real quietly, he whispered. "You take advantage of my crush on you."

"I just want to wear it for a little while," I said. "I promise to take the best of care with it," I said.

I was wearing Jimmy's leather today. It's too big for me, but it smells leathery, and it makes a sound when I lift my arm or put it down. When I wear it no one can touch me. I am safe. Everyone seems to stay a step back from me like I'm something dangerous, which I am. It says how it is—black leather.

Everyone thinks Jimmy and I are lovers.
They don't understand it's that we play guitars.
Playing has to be a family. It has to be like lovers.
The notes have to love the other notes. It can't be
clumsy, like some first wet kiss, like a kiss that
doesn't know any lips but its own. The music has to
know the kiss, the sideways run.

Jimmy doesn't always know how to do the
music kiss, but at least he plays with me, and that's
enough for now.

Dutch Jan in denim disappeared, to Greece someone
said, and on a Sunday in mid-July I stood on the sidewalk
where his drawings had been, listening to a young woman
play the saxophone. She had hair that looked alive, long
brown dread locks with shells and beads woven in. She
wore a worn leather fedora. Her eyes were closed while she
played, but when she opened them I saw their warm, deep

green. Her mini-skirt was made of thin pink silk, and I could see through it to her lovely legs. I sat down under a tree between the squares of sidewalk cement and listened. Pulling my sketch pad out of my guitar case, I drew her, only quickly, the outside lines of her hips, her round nipples, her hat, her hair.

Her name was Elka, and she was a German traveler who was living in Amsterdam temporarily. She had hair under her arms, hair on her legs, and she seemed comfortable in her body like a wild animal, a bear or a dolphin, not uptight and ill from working too much at a job she hated. She could make enough money playing her saxophone on the streets, she told me, to pay for a room in a boarding house, to pay for train tickets.

When she asked me to come back to her flat for dinner, I didn't say no. Of all the offers I had gotten—side trips, cold beers, and bedrooms—none had really sounded like a yes to me but hers. Not for sex—I wanted to draw her.

I followed her to a little market where she bought a loaf of bread. And then we went up three flights of stairs to her little room that had a window overlooking the canal. She smelled like lust, like pure sex.

Her English was good, but her accent was thick.

She had been traveling around northern Europe for about a year: Norway, Sweden, Ireland, Scotland, Wales, and England. As she added spices to the spaghetti sauce, I drew her again, but in more detail. Her skin looked like the softest thing ever invented.

"It's okay?" I asked.

"You didn't ask me when I played."

"We weren't talking when you played," I said.

"So if I am not talking that means I am saying yes to you?"

I smiled at her. She was flirting.

The kitchen where she cooked was small. She shared it with the other boarders, and it was three doors down from her room. A man with scraggily hair and broken glasses came in and got a beer and some cheese out of the refrigerator, while Elka cooked.

In her very small room, we sat on her single bed

with plates of spaghetti on our laps. I threw my sketch pad on the floor, and she picked it up.

"So, I look this good?" Elka asked.

"You look better in real life," I said.

"You're good."

"I'm learning," I said.

We ate our dinner, and Elka talked about the mystical stone circles she'd been to in England. She talked about how many new buildings there are in London, because so many old ones got bombed during the war. Then we talked about going to the Jewish Historical Museum.

"People forget," she said.

"Not forgetting is my problem," I said.

She paused. "Not forgetting the war?"

"It seems like it's everywhere in this city. It spooks

me sometimes. It's like it's full of ghosts."

"It does. It does. I feel this way too. The history seems very present," she said.

"Sometimes that's a problem for me," I said.

"It's not a problem. When there are important things, we shouldn't forget," she said. "Things have to work their way through us slowly."

"Too slowly sometimes."

Elka looked at me. "I know," she said. "There are things."

"Not even traveling works," I said.

"No," she said, "but we can always try."

She picked up the dishes and put them on a small table by the bed, and the room became silent. I watched her body moving slowly. She was not thin or fat; she was round, smooth like honey.

"I want to draw you again," I said. "I've been drawing the statues lately, and that's okay. It's easier, because they don't move, but I want to draw you."

"I move, you know?"

"Maybe you would be still for me, just for a little while."

"You've drawn real people?"

"I've always drawn my family and my-"

"Lovers?"

"Lover," I said.

"Loyal person."

"Can't-forget person."

"What should I do?"

"I want you to take your clothes off." I don't know how I said it, but I did. It just came out.

Elka blushed. "O.K., I'll undress for you, crazy

American girl, but you must promise not to laugh."

I watched Elka slowly take her clothes off. Her skirt landed on the floor in a lofty pile, like a parachute settling to the ground. She placed her hat on the window sill and looked over at me and smiled. I asked her to stand against the wall. I don't know how I got that out either. I asked her to relax, and I drew her, my pencil shaking at first, and then settling. Slowly, I felt depth in the page. I felt the soft curves of her as they came through my fingers. I felt her electricity, her playful, wild energy.

Elka stood still for almost an hour. We were silent. We listened to traffic and a couple having a fight in Dutch and our own thoughts, which were probably louder than anything.

"I feel embarrassed and at ease," she said.

"Let me tell you a story while I work," I said.

"I want to hear your story, Mo. You see my story here. I am naked."

"That doesn't tell me anything," I said, smiling.

"It tells you more than you tell me. Who are your parents?" Elka asked.

"White picket fence," I said.

"What do you mean white fence?"

"It's an American expression for *perfect*."

"Your father, he is businessman? Your mother has the apron?"

"My parents are divorced," I said. "My Dad is a drunken newspaper writer. Actually, there is not a picket fence, not even a real one."

I told Elka about Mom and Hank. "My mother left her husband for her successful college sweetheart."

After a long time, Elka

said, "I can't be naked alone any longer."

I felt heat lightning in my stomach, and slowly put down my pencil. I was trying not to see her like *that*. "I got enough, I think. Thank you. I want to paint this one." I tipped my drawing toward her. I noticed that her lips looked rough and soft, ready for raw kisses.

She glanced at it and quickly looked away. She reached for her shirt. "Oh, my belly. Next time with clothes," she said.

"Your belly is perfect."

In the Spring of my eighth grade year, on April 17, my father gave me an electric guitar for my birthday. It was an Ibanez, and it became Amelia, a name I have told to no one. I named her Amelia because I wanted to fly, whether I made it or not, across an ocean. I wanted to soar across the river to New York City—into a recording studio or even just into the ears of a few close friends. I wanted to try to get off the ground. The concept of musical flight is one I have had from the very beginning. As Jimmy says, "It's in the air." Air and wings. Freedom to be at home in the air, at home where the birds fly, at home in a recording studio.

I have known people who, like me, have wanted to fly, and people who seemed like they could fly. My father's friend Mr. Otten was big and black, almost seven feet tall. His voice was deep. I just remember thinking, POWER. It was like his soul was bigger than his body, and like he would have had the power to take right off if he wanted.

Dad met Mr. Otten at a civil rights meeting in '65, a few years after he and my mom moved to New Jersey. Dad and Mr. Otten went on road trips to Washington, DC to walk. They gave speeches and wrote letters to congressmen.

The Ottens used to come over all the time. They had two kids younger than John and me, Lisa and Tara, and we would have fun cruising around the neighborhood with them when they came to visit, or we would watch movies on television. I remember once Mr. Otten wanted to light the stove, so he turned two burners on and let the gas rise up. He was telling my father a joke, and I remember backing off from the stove, wishing he would get to the end. As he told the punch line, he grinned at my father, struck the match, and threw it in the general direction of the stove. The flames jumped up with the laughter. Mr. Otten's laugh was bigger than the flames, though. He was bigger than the whole house.

It seems like most white people have invisible turtlenecks around their throats. It's not that we don't laugh, it's just that we laugh quieter. I don't want to be quiet about things. I want my flames to jump up.

When my Dad and Mr. Otten got into their fifth martinis, they would be way out of the safety zone, talking about Nixon, and Jackson, and joking about how the chitlins on the back of the stove smelled. Mom and Mrs. Otten would get just as angry about Nixon, but they wouldn't get as drunk, and they'd talk about us kids.

All their gatherings would go on for hours, and Dad and Mr. Otten would end up asleep on the living room floor. They would drift out of a drunken talk on how to change the world into a dialogue of snores. They were best friends.

When Dad gave me the guitar, it was just before Mr. Otten killed himself, shut off his power. That day was May 5th of my eighth grade year. That was the day something big inside my father also died.

I had to do one thing to get the guitar from my father. At my birthday party he was pretty wasted on gin, and he made a pact with me that I could keep the guitar if I did a portrait of him. He had this thing about me painting a picture of him.

I got a canvas, and I painted him. I remember that everything was blooming. He said that it was my time of year because I was born when everything blossomed. That bloom, he sat in the worn-out lawn chair drinking, and I painted him.

Painting a portrait of him was an easy trade, because I wanted to keep my electric. It's not that he would have taken it back, it's just that he needed an excuse to ask me to paint him. So I filled the canvas, and it was him. He had a half smile, the one that's turned into a quarter smile now. His two blue eyes came out perfectly, and his hair came down in a wave just like it does. In the painting he looks like the dentist in "Rudolph the Red-Nosed Reindeer," and he is sitting in the lawn chair with his glass in hand. At first I drew him in pencil, and then I filled him in with paint.

I finished the painting on May 1st. When I told him I didn't need him to model anymore, his words were slurring pretty badly. "Well, my young artist, I guess I'll be heading for the typewriter," he said, staggering across the yard toward another drink.

Two days later, he asked when I was going to get around to doing his portrait. I said that it was already finished, and he said, "I should have some time in a few days." I said again that it was finished. He seriously thought I was joking. He was seriously sober when he said it, not drunk enough to remember. I decided he didn't deserve the painting, so I kept it for myself.

The night Mr. Otten killed himself, I took Elmer's glue and stuck the painting to the inside of Amelia's case. At the bottom of the lawn chair in the painting, in permanent ink, I wrote, "Mo Taylor." I sprayed it with shellac to protect it. I had never even said the name Mo, before that I had always been Molly.

"I want you to draw something ugly, something disgusting, something that makes you feel uncomfortable," Dr. Everitt announced.

So much is ugly. All you have to do is step outside the forest, I thought, *and there are ugly things everywhere.*

"Life is a mixture. Without the interplay of creation and destruction, nothing would move forward."

I raised my hand. "Why can't it just be beautiful? I mean, since there is so much garbage and pollution, why should we focus on drawing something ugly? It's in our faces all the time. Art is how I get away from all of that."

"So you use art to balance out the pain of life with something beautiful?"

"No. I use art to try and make something beautiful in a world that destroys beauty."

"That is a very strong motivation, a strong thought, Mo, but let me ask you something. What is true, the ugly or the beautiful?"

"Both."

"So do you want your art to be lopsided, only half the truth?"

"Life is lopsided, Dr. Everitt. Sometimes there is more of one than the other."

"That is also true. I would just ask you to consider

creating in the middle somewhere, not only to one side. In fact, I believe it is almost impossible not to, especially for someone like you." She raised one eyebrow and looked directly at me. "And, for this assignment, I want you to see the inverse of the situation. I want you to see the beauty of form of the ugly."

Someone like me, what the hell did she mean by that? Dr. Everitt walked up to me and spoke quietly, so that only I could hear her.

"I respect very much that you value nature, but if you see the city as ugly and the country as beautiful, why do you represent yourself as a city person in some ways? Your black clothes, your leather jacket, they are city clothes. It's not black and white, Mo. Nothing is." She spoke loudly enough for everyone to hear her again. "Look inside trash cans. Look for patterns of sludge in the canals. Look at broken glass. Find something horrid and draw it."

Samantha ordered a plate of fries. From the diner, we watched the sun go down behind the turnpike, behind the factories, marshes, and garbage dumps. The sky looked drawn by crayons.

"So you have a crush on anyone, Mo?"

"Not really."

"Come on," she said. "You haven't given in to Jimmy?"

"That's not going to happen. Me and Jimmy play guitars together."

"Who do you like, Mo?"

"What do you want me to tell you, who I look at in the hallways?"

"Yeah, I want to know that."

"Who do you want, Samantha? Why don't you have a boyfriend?"

"You, too, a new girl like you. I'm surprised too."

"Yeah, well, I don't know, the guys are afraid of a girl who plays electric guitar."

"You're right," she said.

"So what scares them about you?" I asked.

"My height...I'm too tall," she said.

"Yeah," I said, "it's that you're too beautiful. That's what's scary."

"Yeah, right," she said. She paused and then said, "I got into two schools."

"That's great, but you know that means we won't get to go out kicking through the leaves together," I said.

She smiled gently, "The University of Virginia and the University of Vermont."

"Where do you want to go?"

"Virginia. It'll be warmer."

"Spring will come sooner there," I said.

That night everything in my room felt rounded and soft with drunkenness and humidity. Samantha and I were alone. There was wine in my tears, and I rubbed my hands down my cheeks to try and stop them.

Samantha moved over and put her arm around my shoulder; it felt like warm bird feathers. She massaged the back of my neck. Then she changed everything forever; she leaned over and kissed a tear that was rolling down my cheek. And then she licked one. She licked it. And then she kissed me.

It was two-thirty in the morning, and I listened to the quiet patter of my black boots on the sidewalks as I walked. *I have an excellent sense of direction,* I thought, as I doubled back. I gripped the sleeves of Jimmy's leather in my hands. Van Eeganstraat. Van Breestraat. Williams Parkweg. Where was Elka's flat? Sweat was running between my fingers when I finally got to her door. I tried to slow my breathing.

Elka had been asleep, but she smiled to see me, and she poured me a glass of wine. We sat on her bed.

I reached into my backpack and pulled out my journal. "I want to read this to you," I said, "to someone besides myself."

"It's the story of your life?" Elka asked, rubbing her eye.

"Some of it," I said. "The sad parts and the sexy parts."

"Read me the sexy," she said. "It will be like you getting naked."

"You want to see me naked?" I asked.

"I want to hear you naked," she said, smiling.

I read Elka the parts I had read to myself, and then I got to the part she wanted to hear:

Adults forget what it's like having everything hit you for the first time. I would never have thought that I could fall in love with a girl, but I can't think of anything else.

Love does not stop at the corner. Love does not stop for red lights. It wakes me up so alive that nothing can put me to sleep. Nothing can stop me.

Love does not stop for innocence because it is innocence. It's pure. It forgets ages. It forgets color and money, and sometimes it even forgets to be a woman and a man.

We walked to the park late last night, after

play rehearsal. She walked around me and put her hands on my back. She made slow circles on my shoulder blades with her fingers.

"I want your hands on me," I said.

I didn't really know where she was taking me, but I was going

"I'm crazy," she told me, and she turned me around. I felt her fingers weave into mine, and her hair brushed my cheek as she leaned in to kiss me on the lips.

Did our kisses know we were kissing?

We were kissing.

We were her long blond hair, and we were kissing. We were rushing.

Did our kisses know we were kissing?

"Hey, Molly, I want you to sleep over tonight," is what she says to me many times, and it

happens many times. All day long it is me. All of
me is Samantha.

One big secret.

We learn how to look at each other without
letting anyone know. Sometimes Samantha
touches me, but I don't let anyone else see. Under
tables. Behind people's backs. Blushes can't
happen; I try to never let them work their way to
my face. I am getting good at hiding what is most
important to me.

It's a gentle love. Gentle like soft skin itself.
Love like soft skin. Love so big it takes over. Before
I was asleep, and now I'm awake. Love is
changing every part of me. Words only come close
to explaining. Crying all night says how I feel, but
not just my sad tears, my everything tears.

Words and love. Words and sex. I feel so
much of me. I feel like the day of the spring bloom.

The music gets it for whole songs, whole chord progressions of Samantha. Whole verses feel like my love for her. Music comes closest to explaining the love, so I play, and play, and play. All day long I kiss the air with the music of my love.

There is nothing perverted about it, nothing wrong, and I knew it from the first rushes. I knew it from the honest love. I know it's right to love her.

The other night, we were in Samantha's bed close to sleeping. Samantha said, "I hate hiding the most wonderful thing in the world." She kissed me. After a few minutes, she said, "You can do whatever you want, Mo."

"I want to," I said.

I fell asleep on Elka's floor as the sun came up, and she fell asleep in her bed. We didn't wake up until 5:00 PM. I missed Dr. Everitt's class. I had not drawn anything ugly.

"Do you not find my class valuable?" Dr. Everitt asked me that night in the studio at the University. I had pulled out my drawing of Elka, and as Dr. Everitt walked toward me, I flipped it over on the desk. I couldn't answer Dr. Everitt; finally I had a teacher that I liked, and I had not done her assignment. I was still wearing the clothes I'd worn the night before; I had wine and cigarettes on my breath from a dinner-breakfast I'd had with Elka. I was contemplating using paint on a drawing pad.

"I've seen the pictures of your paintings that you sent in with your application. You're obviously very gifted," she said. "I gave you a B on your doorway; I handed them back today. You worked on that. Maybe the pace of these assignments is too much for you, or maybe you feel you are too talented to work."

I held still. I stopped breathing.

"Or maybe you are having too much fun partying in Amsterdam." She walked by me, and I could feel the swift, small breeze she created.

"I want to work," I said, finally breathing again.

"You do?"

"Yes." I decided not to care if she smelled the secrets on my breath.

"What are you working on?"

I flipped the paper over, and there was Elka standing naked.

"I see," Dr. Everitt said, glancing at the paints on my desk. "You want to work?"

"What should I do?"

"That's a good question." Dr. Everitt's mind seemed taut and compact like the rest of her, and I could sense the electrical connections firing through her brain. My syllabus was being created. "I want you to design your assignments for the next month," she finally said. "Focus on something with which you will work. It's okay with me if you draw or paint."

I thought, *I will draw Samantha. I will draw her back to me.*

"Draw something new to you," she said offhandedly, or maybe not so offhandedly. "You think about it, present it to me, and I must approve it. You must complete the reading assignments, of course, and pass my quizzes and tests, but the reading doesn't seem to be the hard part for you. Let me know what your ideas are in two days."

"Can I ask you a question?"

"Yes."

"Does it have to be new?"

She paused for a moment. "I don't know. Does it?"

What would I draw if I wasn't drawing Samantha?

Saturday morning I was sitting in Samantha's living room. The Thompson's couch was covered with thick, velvety material. It was soft and comfortable. Samantha's mother was pinning Samantha's costume for the play, and I could hear them in her mother's sewing room.

"Careful, Mom, you're poking me."

"I'm not poking you. Just hold still, you keep squirming."

"Mom, that hurts."

"Oh, Samantha, stop."

"You never listen to me. You really are poking."

I heard the rustling fabric of Samantha's dress.

"Put your costume on young lady. We need to do this so I can finish it. Samantha, the front door is wide open."

Samantha ran into the living room wearing nothing but her underpants. Nothing else. Her arms were folded, covering her breasts.

"Samantha, stop. Come let me pin this dress for you."

"Don't you get it?" Samantha threw her arms down to her sides.

"Come on in the sewing room, Honey. Of course I listen to you. What is it that I don't listen to?" Mrs. Thompson's voice was frantic.

Samantha ran upstairs.

I was eating breakfast in the kitchen alone with Mom.

"Mrs. Thompson and I had a talk on the phone yesterday, and we'd like to know what is going on. We could understand if you two slept over at each other's houses once a month, but lately it's been twice a week. She told me Samantha stayed here the weekends we were away."

I was sinking. It felt like the night I almost drowned in the lake.

"We are really just close friends, Mom."

My mother's face was white with early morning, her long dark hair plastered to her cream covered cheeks.

"We had a long talk, and we decided that the two of you should not sleep over at each other's houses anymore. We decided you should take a

70

little break from one another. Mrs. Thompson said that Samantha hadn't been herself lately, and when I think about it, you haven't been either. You've been rude, talking back to me."

"Why is that, do you both think?" I asked.

"Because both of you are too young to be making these kinds of decisions."

I had drunk too much white wine. I was running down the dock and diving into the moon in the lake water. I dove so far I didn't know which way was the sky.

"How old do you have to be to love somebody?" I asked my Mom.

Her hands were vibrating. The coffee was shaking inside her coffee cup. "It's perfectly fine to love people, Molly, but this kind of behavior is unacceptable to me and to Mrs. Thompson. Whatever it is, you are too young to be making

71

these kinds of decisions."

"It's not a decision, it's a feeling."

"Acting on it is a decision. I want you to know that we have decided not to tell your fathers."

"For Christ's sake, let's not tell the fathers. I hope you mean upsetting Dad, because Hank's not my fucking father." I was so far down. Where was up? I was running up time without breathing.

"Take it easy, Molly, I'm trying to handle this as best I can."

"Why do you have to handle anything? It's my life, Mom."

"Yes, it's your life, but I am your mother. I've lived a little longer, and you need to respect me."

I was reaching into what might have been the shadow of a star, but it was all thick, black lake water. I needed to breathe.

"What about me? Don't I get respect? When will it be time to start respecting me? Will I be twenty-five or maybe thirty? I'll have to have my own kids just to be respected. Okay, Mom, this is what I'll do: I'll grow my hair long, just like yours. I'll find a boyfriend and marry him. You will be happy, Mrs. Thompson will be happy, and Hank will be happy. I'll have eight kids. Then you will be happy. Then maybe you will respect me."

She reached out to slap my face, and I caught her hand in mine.

Water was coming in. In my nose. I was gulping it in. Big sputtering, acid, fighting, clattering my lungs. No more breathing.

"Just go ahead and slap me across the face for loving someone."

"You are grounded for a week, maybe

73

longer. I will not tolerate the tone of voice you're using. Go to your room, Molly Taylor."

I knocked her coffee mug onto the floor really hard, so it broke. I slammed the door hard behind me.

"Molly Taylor!"

I pounded my feet against the steps, and landed in my bed sobbing. "I love her, I love her, I love her," I screamed.

"Move out of the way. Let me take care of her."

Very far away—my brother John, his hands in my armpits, my ribs hit the dock, a punch to my guts, half the night came out of me.

That was a summer ago.
This morning, at
breakfast, my mother
tried to drown me....

I saw Jimmy through his kitchen window.
The steam of the dishes he washed made it look
like he was in a fog. When he unlocked the door
he was still wearing his plastic, yellow gloves.
"Come on," he said, dropping them on the counter
and pushing the door open to the basement.
That's where we play. We can make as much noise
as we want, because his father is always working.

Jimmy built a room for himself, like a fort,
in the corner of his basement. He lugged in wood
and built the walls. Then he lined the walls with

carpet and posters of rock bands. We play in there, and the carpeting sucks up extra noise, so we can hear what we are playing. It smells like dirt and old cement, and we can't leave our guitars in there, because it gets as cold as the ground does at night.

Jimmy picked up his ratty old acoustic and started talking to me through a scale. He's gotten the technicality, but he still can't seem to feel what I'm doing when we play, and I still always end up following. He has memorized some songs, but his notes are still clumsy. His fingers sometimes move like his words, too fast, and then they get jumbled and hard to follow. My fingers get ripped up on my guitar strings when I play with him.

I lit a cigarette and opened my guitar case.

"That picture inside your guitar case looks exactly like your father."

I kicked it closed and threw my guitar strap over my shoulder. "Yeah, I painted it a long time ago. You sound good; you been playing?"

"You love your father?" he asked me.

"What kind of question is that?" I blew out a long deep drag. "Of course I love him."

"Then how come you keep his picture in a box?"

I reached over and opened up the case again. "There. He can watch us play now. You start. Start, Jimmy." Jimmy started to play, expecting me to follow him, as usual, but I reached out, laid my hand on his strings, and he stopped.

"You follow me this time, Jim." I started to play.

And he followed, sort of. I sang, and he

stayed with me. He lost me in spots, he floundered hard, but he came in cool with a few licks. It was fun. We played songs and sometimes just jams. Sometimes I was beyond trying, my fingers detached from my brain, and I just played. That's what I'm after: pure moments of just playing.

"I'm doing okay?" Jimmy asked when we stopped.

"You're doing great."

"Mo, did I ever tell you how I found this bird one day in the rain? He was a baby, and he really couldn't fly, so I let him live here in the room with me. I would go out and dig up some worms for him, crush them, and feed him though an eyedropper. He got to a point where he could sort of fly, down but not up. He would fly from the bed to the floor. One day I came back and he was gone. I tore the room apart to make sure he wasn't stuck under something, and he wasn't. He must have gotten out through my little window, but the thing that sucks is that he never learned to dig up his own worms."

"I bet he figured it out," I said to Jimmy. "You'd been feeding them to him, so he had a taste for them. I bet he sniffed them out."

"You think?"

"I know," I said.

"You are my friend, Mo."

"You too, Jimmy."

"I know why you're sad. I know what it is you miss. I'm not stupid. People think so…."

I looked up at him. "I don't think so," I said.

He was tapping on the side of his head. "I'm going to show you something."

"Okay."

"Listen," he said, "hear that?" He was still tapping his head.

"What?"

"Here," Jimmy said, "put your fingers right here. It's a plate they put in after I had an accident when I was seven."

"Sounds tinny," I said.

"Yeah, I got percussion for this band."

"Yes, you do."

I assumed that Elka would be gone the next time I went to see her, off to India or Prague, maybe Indonesia, but she was still there, reading a novel in her bed.

"What's up?"

"There is a lot up," she said. "The ceiling, the

couple upstairs who are always fighting, the people who live over them; the sky is somewhere up there."

"I have something to ask you," I said. "It's a big thing."

"Better sit down and we better have wine if it's a big thing," she said.

"Okay."

She opened up a new bottle and poured it into the two small glasses from the kitchen. "Does it upset you that I'm a....that I'm a lesbian?" I asked.

She took a sip. "No, it doesn't upset me. Why would it upset me?"

"Because it upsets most people... It certainly upset my mother when she found out."

"Well, I am not most people in the world or your mother."

"That is good. I just haven't known you that long,

and I read you my journal, and it's a naked thing, you know?"

"It's okay, Mrs. Mo. It's okay."

"Mrs. Mo," I repeated. "You are crazy."

"I am not crazy. So is that *the* big thing?"

"No, I mean, that is *a* big thing, but it's not *the* big thing."

"What?"

"I need to make my own assignment for this class I'm taking. I have to draw or paint something or a series of things. I have to figure out what it is I have to draw, and I want it to be you."

"So, I put these things together, and I think you are coming on to me."

"I need a model."

She smiled. "You know, you've never asked me what it is I like."

"What is it that you like?"

"I like men and I like women."

"You do?"

"I'm just talking about your assumptions."

"My ass-umptions."

"Your ass-umptions," she said, and we both smiled and sipped.

"So will you be my model? I can't pay you."

"Do I have to be naked?"

"You can be whatever you want, upside down, backward, dressed, with clothes, with your saxophone, without it, whatever. I want to draw you."

"Okay," she said.

"It means you can't leave town for three or four weeks."

"Why would I leave?" she asked.

"You're a traveler, aren't you; isn't that what you do?"

The next day I told Dr. Everitt, "I want to draw a traveler, the woman with the shells in her hair, she's German."

"She is willing to model for you?"

"Yes."

"Then thirty five drawings or fifteen paintings. Maybe some combination thereof."

Dr. Everitt had a way of silencing me.

"I wouldn't stand there," she said. "You have three and a half weeks. Go work."

It was an unreasonable, almost insane assignment.

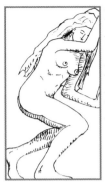

I drew Elka on trains. I drew her sitting on a bridge made out of stones. I drew her playing her sax. I drew her in the middle of people. I drew her standing in an old wooden doorway. I drew her eating a dried fig. I stretched canvasses and stacked them in her room.

In the first scene of the school play, Samantha and I are both onstage. Samantha is a lady of the court, and I am a princess being questioned. Am I worthy enough to marry the prince?

When our drama teacher set up the scene, he explained that we would all have to hold still, our action frozen, while the narrator spoke and filled the audience in on what was happening. "Find a position you can hold." Samantha and I chose to stare into each other's eyes.

When the play opens, we will stand up there in front of everyone and look lovingly at each other for two whole minutes, and all of them will have to sit there watching us, with no way to stop it.

It will be silent, but it will end our silence.

The Stationslein was filled with jugglers, food vendors, and musicians. I saw Elka from a distance playing her sax. As I approached, I saw a small crowd of people surrounded her—travelers and business people. People stopped to put money in her case. She really could play.

I watched her dreads fall back as she dropped her head back. She was absolutely gorgeous.

I put down my case and pulled out my acoustic guitar. Elka looked up and nodded to me invitingly. We had never played together.

We had an hour of perfect music. If playing was kissing, we made love freely in the center of a crowd. Something beyond me played the rhythms around Elka's melodies.

When we stopped, our cases were filled with money.

Elka explained to me that things were heating up a bit politically for a group of squatters in the nearby "Wyers," an old tenement building. I had no idea what she was talking about, so I followed her a few blocks to the old building so she could show me. I was shocked. These people had an entire community built there. There were living places with colorful rugs from Morocco, and floor mats, and futons. There was a coffee shop, a play area for children, and a wood shop where four or five guys were building cabinets and furniture.

As we drank very strong coffee, Elka explained that most of the people in the city supported these squatting hippies who worked very hard to sustain their political statement against capitalism. Elka had two friends who were tailors there. They made cotton clothes that looked like big sacks. The cotton was supposedly grown and picked by people paid fair wages, not those being exploited by U.S. capitalists.

The woman who served us coffee—like all the women there—had hair under her arms and on her legs and a strong, natural body scent.

Under the small table where we sat, Elka's leg bumped up against mine; it was like a soft warm wave on my thigh. I looked at her, raising my left eyebrow, and she pushed her leg up against mine and kept it there.

"I'm sorry," she said. "You are just very beautiful today."

"Are you sure you know what you're doing?" I asked her.

"If I don't know, maybe you will show me," she

said, and I felt her words between my legs.

The world was so fresh to me that day. It was like I
had never seen it before. Everything was a possibility. I
was not locked into anything. I thought about what it
would be like to live in a squatter's community fighting
capitalism. I thought about being with Elka.

"If you want, I'll take you to dinner," Elka said. "We
are rich musicians today."

"I want," I said.

We walked into a quiet residential neighborhood not
far from Elka's flat. The trees and buildings made the street
into a tunnel. I watched Elka skip and then spin on the
sidewalk in front of me, her saxophone case pulling her
around faster and faster. The air was cool enough for
leather, and I wore Jimmy's. My cigarette was glowing in
the night, as wind raced through Elka's clothes bringing the
soft scent of her to me. An old couple walked by, and the
man smiled at Elka's dance-walk. She looked like a person

in love. "This is the place," she said, walking into the front door of a small restaurant.

I took the last drag off my cigarette and walked in behind her.

"What do you think of the drawings so far?" I asked.

"I think they are really good, really good drawings. They are making me feel beautiful."

"You are very," I said.

"This best good feeling I have for you," she said, maybe the intensity of her feelings breaking up her English sentence. Elka looked at me with a seriousness I had not seen her wear before. "Thank you," she said.

"What do you mean?" I felt fear deep and undeniable somewhere in my stomach.

"I was someone's heartbreak back in Germany. I wasn't what someone wanted me to be."

"A lover?" I asked.

"A wife."

It took me a moment to be able to speak. I couldn't help laughing just a little. "You were married?"

"Yes. Why does it seem impossible to you?"

"I have never known anyone who was married, a friend, I mean.......How old are you? I've never asked you that. How could you have done all of this already?"

"I have done all of this, and I am thirty. I am thirty and wandering." She looked down.

"How long were you-"

"Five years."

"Five years. All this time I've been telling you about myself, about the things I've lost, and now I feel so stupid for not listening."

"You're not stupid. You make me be in my life, not

somewhere back there."

"I make you able to forget," I said.

"Best kind of traveling."

The café, the cheese on the top of the onion soup, the thin loaf of warm bread, the white summer wine, the door to her room, the voices outside, the night. I don't know when it was that we actually started touching, somewhere at the end of one of our sentences. It was a place where nothing needed to be written down, because everything that we wanted was there.

The shadows of us on the wall did not sleep. We did not stop until I had to leave for class the next day, with the smell of her on my tongue and fingers.

So long I have kept the love hidden, swallowing it up like dry fear on my tongue.

It seems evil, how they can say I'm sick for loving someone? They write it off as a stage.

Why don't they ever just get it? It has to do with loving somebody. It has to do with seeing beauty, and wanting to be beautiful. It is love.

"Curl your long hair; love dolls and strollers. Don't worry if you notice that your throat squeezes in. Forget yourself if you can't breathe."

It's like explaining ghosts to a person who has never seen one. It is something that only the secrets of your experience can teach you—if you allow yourself to tell yourself the truth, and if you can send your fear out walking long enough to understand what some people feel when they fall in love.

I was stopping back at my dorm to get some clothes on my way to the studio when I got the letter:

Dearest Molly,

Being home this summer, I have been visiting all your favorite trees. I've climbed the one in my backyard every day. I imagine you in Amsterdam. I'm afraid you'll travel off and never return. It wouldn't surprise me. I know the woman you are and the one I imagine you'll become.

I want to be with you, my dear.

I want you back, Mo.

I love you,

Samantha

"Lighten up," Samantha said, right after she told me she was with Ian. "Music is your life. If it's not Jimmy, you'll find someone to fill in the rhythm spaces for you. I can feel it. You're gonna cut the record business to shreds one of these days."

Samantha left because it was her time; she's a year older than me. One month after she left, she was in Professor Ian Carpenter's bed letting him fuck her.

The letter I received in Amsterdam, her new words, felt like a favorite necklace I had been looking for, one that had been lost for a whole year. But when I found it, it was tarnished, and when I put it on my neck, it didn't feel like mine anymore. It felt wrong. How could that be? She was all I thought about.

The whole year after Sam left, I was wrapped up in the loss of her. That's why I clung so hard to my music. I felt like it was all I had. I had tried to love her and she not only left, but she found another lover before the leaves froze. For a long time I didn't even really care about that, I just missed her. I wanted to be with her.

I tried to get the image of her face in my mind. I couldn't concentrate, so I picked up my pad with all the drawings of her off my desk. It had found its place amidst my art history books. I had always gone back to my drawings to see her. I looked through them carefully, turning the pages slowly, letting my tears drop on the pages.

I rolled up the drawings and stuffed them in a cardboard mailing tube that I bought at the university book store. I could feel their weight along the muscles of my arm and shoulder as I walked to the campus post office.

"I think about living somewhere that's alive. I want to have a bedroom with big windows that will be open all summer long. The air will be the wallpaper... If you could go anywhere in the world, where would it be?" I asked Elka.

"To live or to go?"

"Either."

"I want to see the statue of Sappho on Lesbos," she said without thinking.

I laughed. "You're just saying that to make me laugh or to please me."

"No, I really mean it. I studied her work in college and I think it's beautiful," Elka said.

"I haven't read her poems yet, but I've seen pictures of those islands. I think the most perfect places on earth are the places where the mountains meet the ocean."

"I like the white adobe houses and the sidewalk

stairways that wind through the marketplaces."

"You've been there?"

"No, not yet. Only in the films."

"Me only in the films too," I said.

I had stacked seven canvases against Elka's wall, and I pulled one out and held it in my hands. I looked over at her; she was stretched out on her bed looking up at the ceiling. "You're getting tired of this," I said.

"Tired of you drawing me?"

"Yes."

"No, I'm not tired of it," she said. "I am not a perfect beauty."

"You are perfect for me," I said.

Elka jumped up, locked the door to her room, and sat back on the bed. She cupped her breasts with her hands.

"Wow," I said. "You are not making me want to

draw you, you're making me want you."

She pulled off her worn green t-shirt and unhooked her bra with paisley patterns on it. She pressed her breasts up gently. "Draw."

I picked up a canvas and did what she said. I started with her face. I drew her beaded hair, her shells, her eyes, her cheek, nose, and lips. I had to erase her chin one time and I drew it over. I did the curves of her shoulders and the bends in her elbows; I slowly drew the outline of her breasts. She let me touch her when I wasn't sure of a line. She let me see the soft fullness of her breasts, big and round. Her nipples. Her belly.

The silence grew around us, and my mind was still. These flowing lines. This perfect woman. A summer night in Amsterdam.

My drawing hand started feeling weak, and I could feel my belly getting hot and tight. Tears slid down my cheeks, and I placed the canvas on the floor next to the others. My passion dissolved into awe, into confusion, into sadness. My sobs started to roll like waves, small at first then bigger and bigger.

I sat on the edge of the bed and Elka sat behind me, wrapping her legs around my legs, pressing her breasts into my back, holding me tightly with her arms like an anchor.

"I mailed all the drawings I ever did of Samantha back to the States today."

I could feel Elka's body get rigid but she still held on to me.

"They're probably sitting in some crate at the airport or some customs guy is jerking off to them." I thought of drawing them, of the times that Samantha had trusted me the way Elka was trusting me now.

"I feel like I'm betraying both of you by drawing you like this." I couldn't stop crying. "I feel like I want to break all my pencils and rip up all my drawings. It always felt so right, like it was one of the things that was saving me, and now it feels all wrong, it feels ugly."

I could feel Elka pull back, and when I turned around she had tucked her knees into her chest. "Maybe it's me that's wrong," she said.

"No. Don't do this. I'm just having some sort of crisis; it doesn't have anything to do with you. I think I love you."

My words hung in the air.

"I don't need think," she said. "I don't need half a heart."

"I have a whole heart," I said.

"Not yet, you don't. It was not supposed to get like this."

"What do you need?" I asked.

"I need you to go. I need to be alone," she said, placing her hand in the center of my upper chest and pushing me slowly and solidly out the door.

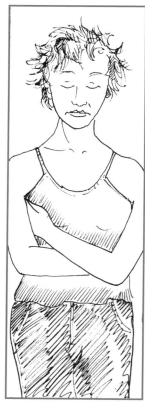

The inside of her room sounded hollow and empty, as I knocked on her door after class the next day. "Come on, Elka, let me in, I just want to talk to you."

The older guy with the broken glasses, who lived on her floor, came out into the hallway. I noticed how long and thin his bare feet were, and that every end on all of his hairs looked split. "She's gone," he said, taking a slug of Heineken. I realized this guy was an old hippie, probably from Nebraska or Ohio, that would never find his way home. "Took her backpack and her saxophone this morning and left. Has her place paid until the end of August; maybe she'll be back." He looked at me kindly, and I realized for the first time that someone else besides Elka and me knew we had been together.

"You think she might come back?"

"I hope so," he said, turning and walking down the hall.

Inside her room there was nothing left but the bed and chest of drawers that belonged to the boarding house, and my undrawn canvases propped up against the wall next to the window. I looked for the one I had drawn on the night before, the only naked one since that first day, but it was gone. She must have pulled the nails out, rolled it up, and taken it with her, because I found the wooden frame next to the refrigerator in the kitchen.

I didn't run anywhere. My body felt like it was filled with baking flour, or rocks, or cement, so I just slowly walked, lugging my body with me. I moved without thinking about what I was going to do next. I moved mechanically, because I was afraid to stop.

Childhood left the day Mr. Otten killed himself. My father's best friend put a gun in his pocket, walked out the front door, past his wife and kids, to the community swimming pool. He stood on the diving board and shot himself in the head, filling the deep end with blood.

My father's face was dull and pale when he walked into my room and sat at the edge of my bed. He looked old, like in one day he'd aged ten years.

"Molly, Albert killed himself. He shot himself." At that moment he really started crying. My father cried, and I put my arms around him.

My childhood left that day. My dad never really came back to live with us after that.

Spin, spin, jabber, jabber, they all came in, and they were stomping and pounding. It was

battle time, and they dug in the stomping rhythm.
I had to find some place to hide from them, so I
went little - I was in Mommy's and Daddy's big
brass bed with John, and we were pretending it
was a boat. Sharks' fins circled us in the water.
The stuffed animals were piled high, and we were
climbing to the top of them. I rolled down and I
hung off the bedpost. John was pulling hard to get
me back on board. He was safe on the big blue
quilt.

Is it Thursday, or Wednesday, or I seemed to
have thought it was Friday. Jabber, jabber, jabber.
What day is today?

"I've got to talk to you, Honey. Come outside
and talk."

My dad showed up at our door stumble-
drunk. The temperature had dropped below thirty,
and my hair was wet from a shower, but I went

outside on the porch with him anyway. We sat on the porch swing. My ankles and my toes hurt I was freezing so badly.

Dad ran his hand over the top of my head. "I am so sorry," he said. "I am sorry for this nightmare."

I sat out there with him until I wasn't cold anymore. And then he got into his car and drove away. My dad doesn't live with us anymore.

You push me right out of my own home.

Heart home.

I thought you were my heart home.

I want to go home.

After Elka left, I tried to work on the drawings of her, finish them for Dr. Everitt. I felt like I had felt playing guitars with Jimmy. Everything was awkward, but I kept going.

A few days after Elka left, there were two more letters from Samantha. I lifted one of them up, trying to make out the words through the envelope, but all I could make out was "and the other."

I put the letter down before I opened it, and I thought of Elka. Why had I let myself get so close to her? I had known she would disappear; she was a traveler, that's what she was. I had spent a year missing Samantha; that was all I had done. Now she was offering herself to me, and I didn't know what I loved more, Samantha or missing her. It was a big part of who I had become, and as I looked at the second unopened letter I realized I wanted to be more than that.

"It's Saturday, Mo," Dr. Everitt said. "How did you find my apartment?"

"A student of yours who was in the studio told me where you live; I hope that's okay. I think his name is Ralph. I guess I looked sort of desperate to him, or something, because he said I should see you" I had a folder with my drawings of Elka in it under my arm.

"It's okay," she said, nodding at the mention of Ralph. "Come in."

Inside Dr. Everitt's apartment, paintings covered almost every inch of all the walls. She led me into the living room. The air was very warm outside, and her windows were open. She showed me her studio, which was a glassed-in room which she had built onto the back of her apartment. There were plants and pots everywhere. I realized that she was not just a visiting professor; she lived there.

"You work for Branston?"

"I used to be on staff there. I came here to teach one summer and I never left."

"Wow."

"I'm the coordinator of the summer program. And I teach art, of course." A formality remained with her, even though I was in her home.

Dr. Everitt gave me iced mint tea in her kitchen, which was also overtaken by plants, dusty spice racks, and dirty coffee mugs; her home had an entirely different personality than the rest of her. It was more relaxed. I was beginning to understand some of her layers.

"This is what you've been working on?" she asked.

I handed her my work.

"You two have worked together on these images?"

"We did." I felt exposed. The only naked picture was the one I had drawn of Elka standing up against her wall the day we met, but I felt like I was naked showing them to Dr. Everitt.

When she glanced up at me, she caught me blushing. She closed her eyes and rubbed her forehead. "I can see you have been listening to me, you have taken what I've been teaching you and added it to your work. These drawings look really different than the ones you did at the beginning of the summer."

"Thank you," I said.

"Thank you for letting me see them; I understand that sometimes it's hard to say out loud what one is feeling." She spoke slowly and carefully, "And sometimes it is through one's art that one can first speak to the world."

"See, that's the thing," I said, "I don't know if I can speak this way anymore."

"Sometimes we speak however we can, Mo."

"I just don't know if it's the right way for me anymore. It's too tangled up in people."

"I see," Dr. Everitt said.

"I used to think it made me closer, and now I think that it's a gap, a space between me and the people I love that we can fall into."

"I always say, 'Draw, and draw, and draw. Paint, paint, and paint.' That's what I always say to my students, but, Mo, you know what your relationship is to your art. Sometimes it's just as strong as a love with a person."

"Yes."

She watched me carefully. "Sometimes we need breaks."

"My life just seems so much bigger than my art right now."

"Then live."

I left the twenty-three drawings I had done of Elka with Dr. Everitt, afraid I would never complete the last twelve. But it didn't seem to matter at that point whether I ever picked up a pencil or a paintbrush again.

I was starting to think about what it would be like brushing my teeth with Samantha, cooking meals, sleeping in the same bed together at night. Would that be going backward or forward?

I imagined Elka drinking coffee at a snack bar on a train making new plans with other travelers just met. I saw her in my mind, walking confidently off of a train and into one of those stations with the glass roofs, her sax case swinging back and forth beneath her hand, her fedora, her mini skirt. I called her name once to the empty dormitory hallway, and my voice echoed back to me, "Elka."

"I support your music," Dad said to me in the pizza parlor. "I bought you your guitar."

It's the first time I've seen him sober in a year.

"I know, Dad. I love my guitar. That's the point."

"I also want you to have an education."

"I want to play music. I understand what you want for me, but you need to understand what I want for myself," I said. "I want to play music, not study music theory in a classroom."

"At least try it for one year," Dad said. "Take some art classes."

"No." I thought about how he didn't remember me painting the portrait of him.

"Your grades are good, and you don't even try. Imagine what you could do. Imagine what you could learn," Dad said.

"What about my friend Jimmy? What's gonna happen to him on graduation day? His mind works differently than everyone else's, but he's smart and he should go to college. Last week in his shop class, he took apart a car engine and put it back together, but his dad can't afford to send him to college, so he'll do what he can already do. He'll become a mechanic."

"What's that got to do with you?"

"I can't just go 'cause Hank has money. I've got to want to go."

"He may not be willing to pay for your education in five years, and he is now," Dad said. "I talked to your mother. She says he told you this."

"That's my problem, isn't it?"

"No, choices have consequences," he said. "This could affect your freedom later. What if you are not successful right away? You need food for yourself and electricity for your guitar. You can earn the money for that doing something else you like to do."

"Like art? It's the same as music."

"You could become a graphic artist. I'm just saying you might need a day job, not forever, but for a while, something to fall back on."

"I'm gonna play my guitar."

Dad had a plastic shopping bag with him, and he reached into it. He placed three college applications next to my slice of pizza. Branston, Albridge, and Fischer. All of them were in the mountains down south. All of them had good arts programs for small schools.

I had no more words. It was the first real thing he'd tried to do for me in three years, so I sat there and filled out every piece of paper he put in front of me.

Five days after Elka left there was a knock on my dorm room door. When I opened it and saw Elka standing there, the rest of the world disappeared.

She came into the room and closed the door behind her. She talked slowly. "I was first in Milan, then Venice." She pushed me, her hand pressing up against my chest, guiding me like she had the day she kicked me out, but this time I ended up with my back against the door.

"I didn't think you would come back," I said.

"I needed to be sure I could come back without coming back." She was pressed her body against mine, and I could feel her weight and her soft curves meet mine, breasts against breasts. Her thigh slid in between mine. She kissed my neck.

I wanted to just go and keep going, so it was a struggle to pull myself back, but her comment was beneath her kisses, and I needed to know what it meant. "What do you mean come back without coming back?" I asked.

"Just let me touch you, please." Her eyes were closed.

"Tell me," I said.

She leaned in and kissed me again, her tongue like sex.

This time I pushed her back, my breath hard and rhythmic.

"It means," she said, "that whatever you do, I will be okay with it."

My class was about to end. I had a plane ticket to J.F.K. and an old girlfriend waiting for me.

"Okay," I said, "but I didn't like it when you left."

"I am here now," she said.

I kissed her this time. I took her breath. I took my own. I couldn't stop it.

"I know a Dutch artist named Laurens," Elka said. "He lives outside of Alkmaar, a small town to the north of Amsterdam. There are sand dunes nearby and sea all around. He makes sculptures out of long cuttings of summer grass. I think we should visit him. It's a short bus trip."

During my last week in Amsterdam I would have followed Elka anywhere. I was often truly weak in the knees; they had a sensation inside them sometimes when I walked that felt like outer space was inside my legs. Sometimes I had to sit, and sometimes let Elka hold my hand in public if the place felt safe, like when we went for coffee in the squatter's building.

The day we went to Alkmaar, Elka was wearing a burgundy velvet dress; she looked like a Celtic goddess. When we got there we walked two miles down a road and another mile into a field. At the end of the field stood an enormous snake-like creature. The drying summer grasses formed a sphere, out of which emerged a long, tail-like tube.

No one was there but us, and it was very quiet. "Where's your friend?"

"He'll come when the sun goes down; there's going

to be a celebration here tonight."

"It's hard to imagine people here; it's so quiet."

Elka took a slow breath of the cool foggy air. She closed her eyes and pushed her hat against her head with her hand.

I looked back at the sculpture. "How's it held together?" I asked.

"Woven branches. A month ago it was just a skeleton. It was beautiful that way too."

"It's amazing now."

You could enter the "body" from either end. I followed Elka on my hands and knees deep into the tail of the sculpture. It smelled like sweet grass and cool wet air. I reached out and grabbed Elka's bare legs as she crawled in front of me.

"Stop. You make me feel like I'm being chased, and I was falling on my dress before this." Elka pulled her dress up and wound it into itself around her waist.

"I like to make you feel like you're being chased," I said, lunging toward her.

"No, stop it," she said strongly.

She stopped for a moment, and I rested my hand on her calf, rubbing her lower leg gently. "It's just me," I said.

When she started forward again, she crawled more slowly. I was very close behind. She moved slowly enough that I could feel her upper legs, her thighs and her hips with my fingers, as we went.

In the large round room of straw, the scent of the earth rose up, as I slowly I moved my fingers down toward the center of her.

There was a party that night. We smoked hash and drank beer. People spoke in Dutch, German, and English, and, because there was no music, I listened to the patterns of their voices and the silent night behind them. It was as if I could hear the voice of the ocean behind it all, the vast water so close to us. I was glad we had left our instruments in town, because our playing might have covered up what we heard.

I don't remember falling asleep, but I must have, because sometime just before dawn, I woke up and slipped out from underneath the blanket that had covered me and Elka, and I crept out into the dew-drenched grass and lit a cigarette.

Laurens, who was a tall, blond, really friendly guy, stood up and walked through the middle of his sleeping friends to the sculpture that had taken him three months to build. He dowsed the whole thing with kerosene. I watched him quietly, taking in the scent. When he struck the match, I wanted to leap out and grab it from him. When it hit the sculpture it exploded into tall flames. The heat and the roar woke everyone up. People stood up, rubbing their eyes; some of them panicked.

"Get water."

"Oh my God."

Laurens walked over with a smile on his face, standing between the fire and his friends, "I did this!" he said. "I did it."

Elka gave me back the canvas I'd drawn, and I re-stretched it and nailed it into a different frame. I painted it at the university, and when I couldn't work on it anymore, one of my classmates lent me her bicycle, and I peddled over to Elka's. When I knocked on her door it was 2:30 AM.

"Sorry I woke you," I whispered. Elka held her door open only a crack. Light made a stripe down her naked body. She brushed the hair out of her face.

I got as close to her as I could, the door still only

cracked open between us. "That is sexy," I said. "Can I come in?"

"You said you were going to work all night."

I threw my head back and let out a fast puff of air. I pivoted my body so my back faced the wall next to her door, and I sank down into a sit and pulled my knees up to my chest.

Elka went back into her room, wrapped a blanket around herself, and came into the hallway. "I let a friend spend the night in my room," she said. "He was going to leave here tonight, I mean, he is an old friend traveling back to his city. I just don't want to wake him up."

"Friend? Fuck, I'm getting out of here. I shouldn't have come. I only thought we were lovers, or something. We had a good time, a really good time."

"Mo."

"What?"

She was gripping the blanket tightly around her. "I never meant to hurt you."

"No. I understand. I backed away first."

She paused. "It's true. You did. Still, I'm sorry," she said, as I walked down the hall not looking back. When I walked out the front door, there was city. I kicked a metal garbage can that was sitting in the walkway, and an empty beer bottle smashed inside it and glass flew in the air. Pain ran up the leg I had used to kick. I limped all the way back to the university.

At around nine last night, Dad rang the doorbell and Hank let him into my room to say good-bye. I was getting ready to play Amelia, my electric, for the last time all summer, and my guitar case was lying open in the middle of the floor.

"You got everything all set, Mol?"

"Yeah, just got to put my art stuff in this suitcase."

He looked down at my guitar case, and for the first time, it registered.

"Jesus Christ, Mol, you did a great portrait of me."

I looked up at him. "I know you don't really remember, but you sat for me. It was just before Mr. Otten died."

"I don't remember. There are a lot of things I don't remember." He was still looking at himself in the lawn chair. "I'm sorry."

I knelt down and ripped the painting out of the case. I wrote on the back: Dad, I love you always, Molly. "I should have given it to you a long time ago," I said. "I guess the real reason I kept it was that I wanted you with me."

Samantha took her clothes off. First her t-shirt, then her jeans. Her long hair rested on her shoulders and her breasts. She stood still for a moment, and then she undid her bra and dropped it. She slid her underwear over her hips and dropped them on the pile. She got into my bed and pressed her whole body against mine.

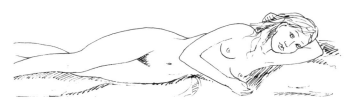

I didn't say anything. I touched all the places I had drawn, all the places to which she said "yes."

At 5:15 AM. I went to Jimmy's house.

"Wake up, man, I want to say good-bye to you."

"What the hell time is it?"

"5:30 AM."

"How did you get in?"

"Your back door was unlocked."

"Where are you going again?"

"Amster-fucking-dam, man."

"Amsterdam."

"I want you to take care of my electric while I'm gone. The amp's here anyway." I put down my guitar case in the middle of his dirty clothes which were strewn all over the floor.

"No kidding. Really? You trust me."

"As much as you trust me with your jacket."

"You stole that jacket, you swindled it. That jacket's not mine anymore."

"Yes it is. I'll give it back to you someday."

"Yeah, when my hair is gray, and I'm wearing tweed suits."

"Sooner than that, Jimmy."

We hugged each other, awkward and strong.

"I'm gonna learn how to play Metal, Mo. Your music is too soft for me."

"When I get back you can teach me your Metal licks."

He nodded. "I'll see you."

"Yeah. See you."

I took a cigarette off the table next to his bed, lit it, and climbed the stairs.

In caterpillar-hood

*We wove strings around each other's
wings –*

Now buttering

Each other to

Fly

I walked toward the train station with my backpack
and my guitar. I had enough money for a train ticket to
Athens, and I figured I could play my guitar for room and
board like Elka. It probably wouldn't take me too long to
earn the money for a boat ticket to Lesbos, and I knew
things would be a lot less expensive in Greece.

Standing in line, I saw a family walk by; the oldest
boy was big and awkward, and he reminded me of Jimmy.
The kid walked like Jimmy, with a similar bob in his step. I

thought of Jimmy sitting in his dark basement playing my guitar, alone most of the time. I thought of him getting a job in a gas station as a mechanic. I realized that I had never ever seen his father, and I had never asked exactly where his mother had gone.

My thoughts became a kaleidoscope of the people I loved and the things I'd done. I thought of my mother's journal, her stories, the perfectly planted flowers in her garden placed so that something would always be blooming all summer long. I thought of my brother John and how he looks like me, all crazy haired and wide eyed, how he hates Hank but loves him like I do, and how Dad leaving wrecked him too. I closed my eyes and imagined my father's face. I imagined Samantha, both of us old ladies rocking on our porch swing. I thought of Laurens torching his sculpture. I thought of sending my drawings of Samantha home to her. I thought of music.

"Hello, miss. Are you next in line?"

It was not time for my trip to Lesbos. I turned and walked slowly and steadily back toward the university.

I went to the zoological museum and drew bats, birds, whales, and bones for two whole mornings on all the blank canvases. Then I took them back to the university and worked on them. Sometimes, painting felt mechanical to me. There were ten new ones, and I spent most of my time working on them. I drank lots of cappuccino and smoked at least a pack of cigarettes a day. I was like a robot filling out a production order. Numbing myself out was the only way I could finish.

At one point I worked for three days solid. I never bathed. I didn't change my clothes. I barely ate. I slept for short stints on the studio floor, woke up and worked again.

The other students would come and go and whisper things to each other about me like "obsessed," or "insane," or "kiss ass." I had not painted or drawn as much as Dr. Everitt had told me to, so I knew I wasn't a kiss ass. But she also told me to live, and I had done that part of the assignment; that, as I'm sure she knew, had been the hardest part. I had also done the other course work she had assigned. She told me it didn't matter if I worked on old things, but I wondered if she knew that allowing me that freedom would push me toward new things.

I finished the painting of Elka last, and I gave that and the rest of my work to Dr. Everitt.

Elka and I were both getting what we felt like we deserved: to be missing someone. No one was there to hurt us. I was used to that. It worked.

Together, Dr. Everitt and I rolled the canvases and drawings and tubed them for me to carry on the plane. I looked at the drawings I had done of Elka. The quick sketch I had done while she was playing her saxophone the first day I saw her was the one I liked the best. Dr. Everitt ended up giving me a B in the class, which I was pleased with, knowing she didn't give A's, even to those who deserved them. I left my home address with Dr. Everitt, and I let her know that if Elka ever came looking for me it would be fine to pass on my address.

It got very cool and gray the day before I left, like the fog was covering all of Holland. As I walked along the street, I pulled up the zipper on Jimmy's leather. I tucked my hands under the straps on my day pack to try and keep them warm.

I wandered slowly to the canal, one block over from where Elka had stayed. I stood on the stone bridge where I had kissed her. I looked at the shop fronts. I listened to the conversations going on around me in Dutch. I had become very at home there. I thought about coming back. I thought about going to see Sappho's statue, after reading her poetry.

I went into the building and up the stairs to Elka's room.

Half way up the stairs I met the old hippie guy, who seemed to have made that boarding house his home.

"Hey."

"Hi," he said. "She's gone for good this time, I think," he said.

"Could you wait just a second? I want to give you my address to give her if she ever comes back."

"Okay."

I pulled off my backpack, ripped a blank page out of the end of my journal, and wrote out my address. "Hey, what's your name anyway?"

"It used to be Ralph, but my friends call me Rat."

"My name's Mo," I said.

"I know. Elka told me."

I handed him the piece of paper. "Thanks. Good luck to you."

"You too," he said, looking like he wanted to say more to comfort me, but he couldn't find the words.

I walked the rest of the way up the stairs into the empty room and looked around. *We made love in here,* I thought.

I walked out of Elka's room, out of her building, down more streets, and beyond the Station Centraal. I walked to the edge of the Het Ij. There was a boat full of tourists going on their tour of the canals, despite the weather, and I watched them

pass. There were a few brave sailors navigating their boats in the foggy wind. I sat at the edge of the water; the wet air tossed around my hair, and the mist covered my face like cold sweat.

As I walked out of customs at J.F.K., I saw Samantha standing there waiting, next to my brother John. My parents would have been there, but John was the only one I had told when I would land.

Samantha's cheeks flushed, as I came up to her. I hugged her really gently. Her hair smelled like sweet shampoo. "You're so skinny," she said, touching my waist.

"I am? I haven't noticed."

"You look great," she said.

"So do you."

I walked over to John and hugged him tightly. "You told her."

"She forced me to tell her."

"It's good to see you," I said, kissing him on the cheek. "Give me a minute to talk to her. You didn't drive out here together, did you?"

"No. I went into the city first."

"Okay."

I walked back over to Samantha.

"Hey," she said.

"Hi. It's really nice of you to come out here to see me come in and all. It's really nice."

"It's good to see you, Molly. You never wrote me back, and you sent me all those drawings, and I didn't know what you were trying to say to me, but it made me really sad. I had to see you. I really, really wanted to see you."

"I can't do this, Samantha. I'm going to Virginia to school next week," I told her.

"I'm going to transfer there, to Branston," she said.

"You can't," I said, my own words surprising me. "Maybe we can visit each other. It's just that I need to be with myself without missing anybody for a change."

"I never really left you," Samantha said, "not in my heart. I'm sorry it felt like that. I'm sorry I hurt you, Molly."

"It's all right. I'm okay."

Samantha ran her fingers down my cheeks. "I still love you," she said.

I kissed Samantha on the cheek and walked toward my brother.

Juli Jousan originally wrote *Drawing Love* by hand in high school and college in notebooks and on napkins. She edited the work by cutting the paper with scissors and laying it out on her front porch. When she was satisfied with how the pieces fit together, she used Scotch tape to bind them into place. Eventually the story made it to an old typewriter. A few years later, it reached a computer.

When she wrote the first drafts of *Drawing Love*, it was the eighties, and most of the world was not ready for a sexy lesbian novel about teenagers. "Did our kisses know we were kissing?" Mo wrote these lines in her journal. Even she, the one who was doing it, wondered if she could admit the truth of what was happening to herself. How could she be kissing another girl? How could her soft lips be pressed up against another girl's soft lips? How could that perfectly amazing thing be happening? Why would people want her to hide this? How could invisibility be immediately demanded of such a natural love?

The world certainly did not know that Juli Jousan had been kissing her high school girlfriend, nor did her teachers or most of her friends. The world would certainly not have imagined that they did more than kiss. If they had found out, they would have called it an experimental phase, or they might have blamed it on her parent's divorce, or the hippies, maybe rock music.

When Juli told her mom that *Drawing Love* was being published, her mom said, "Maybe the world is ready for it now. Maybe things have changed enough."

It is in the spirit of this change that *Drawing Love* is now presented. Much thanks goes out to the lesbian writers who have been brave enough to write letters, books, and academic pieces that have helped to get us here.

Juli is the author of two other novellas and several children's stories. She spent the last decade working with troubled teens. She has led extended trips in the outdoors and traveled throughout the world. She loves to walk and spend time with her friends. She lives in the Finger Lakes region of New York. It is her hope that her books will turn the reader's inner pages and help people to be free enough to be themselves, no matter what their sexual orientation.

Juli has been known to wear cool shoes. Her favorites are her purple sneakers. Her hero is a 90 year old woman who can still bend over at the waist to check if the biscuits are done.